Pocket Cats·

Lucky Star

www.davidficklingbooks.co.uk

Pocket Cats

Lucky Star

Kitty Wells

David Fickling Books

OXFORD · NEW YORK

31 Beaumont Street
Oxford OX1 2NP, UK

POCKET CATS 5: LUCKY STAR
A DAVID FICKLING BOOK
978 1 849 92029 2

Published in Great Britain by David Fickling Books,
a division of Random House Children's Books
A Random House Group Company

This edition published 2010

1 3 5 7 9 10 8 6 4 2

Text copyright © Lee Weatherly, 2010
Inside illustrations copyright © Dynamo Design Ltd, 2010

The right of Lee Weatherly and Dynamo Design Ltd to be identified as the author
and illustrator of this work has been asserted in accordance with the
Copyright, Designs and Patents Act 1988.

The Random House Group Limited supports the Forest Stewardship Council (FSC),
the leading international forest certification organization. All our titles that are printed
on Greenpeace-approved FSC-certified paper carry the FSC logo. Our paper
procurement policy can be found at www.rbooks.co.uk/environment.

Mixed Sources
Product group from well-managed
forests and other controlled sources
www.fsc.org Cert no. TT-COC-2139
FSC © 1996 Forest Stewardship Council

DAVID FICKLING BOOKS
31 Beaumont Street, Oxford, OX1 2NP

www.kidsatrandomhouse.co.uk
www.rbooks.co.uk

Addresses for companies within The Random House Group Limited can be found at:
www.randomhouse.co.uk/offices.htm

THE RANDOM HOUSE GROUP Limited Reg. No. 954009

A CIP catalogue record for this book is available from the British Library.

Printed and bound in Great Britain by CPI Bookmarque

The *Pocket Cats* series is dedicated to all cat lovers, everywhere . . . including you!

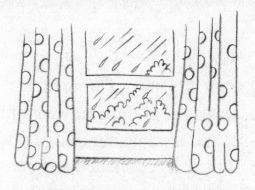

Chapter One

It was a dull Saturday morning in March. Maddy Lloyd sat at the window, gazing out at the grey, dripping world. Nothing the tiniest bit interesting had happened for weeks and weeks now. It almost felt as if nothing interesting would ever happen again.

If Maddy didn't know better, she would have thought she'd dreamed the magic that had been a part of her life since last September. But she hadn't. Upstairs, sitting on her desk, was a set of three tiny ceramic cats . . . and as amazing as it seemed, each of the cats could actually *come to life*, if there was a problem that needed solving.

Maddy sighed, and tucked a strand of her long brown hair behind her ear. She'd had some incredible adventures with the cats, but it had been months since the last one, Greykin, had come to life. *Months*.

Lucky Star

Maybe the magic's finished now, she worried, staring out of the window. She shivered at the thought of never seeing her wonderful feline friends again. No, it couldn't be! Surely Greykin would have said something if that was the case?

But he hadn't. In fact, he'd said practically the opposite, and had promised that her next adventure would be an especially interesting one. Maddy propped her chin on her hand. He hadn't said *when*, though. Perhaps it would be years.

"Maddy, stop moping," chided her mother from the dining table, where she sat reading one of her textbooks. "Isn't there anything you can do? Go and play with Jack, or something."

Maddy made a face. Jack was her little brother, and almost certain to be engrossed in his stupid monster cards. "Maybe I'll text Rachel," she said, getting up slowly. Rachel was her best friend, and the only other person who knew about the cats. She'd understand exactly how Maddy felt. She was desperate for them to come to life again too.

Just as Maddy started to turn away from the window, she saw a bright yellow removals van coming up the road. Behind it was a sleek black car with tinted windows. She paused, watching as the car pulled into the drive next door. The van drew up at the kerb.

"Mum! I think someone's moving into the Bennetts' old house," said

Maddy, peering round the curtain to see.

Looking glad to have an excuse to leave her studies, Maddy's mother joined her at the window. "Oh yes, it was sold a few weeks ago. I wondered who our new neighbours would be."

The two of them watched as a woman with silvery-blonde hair cut into a neat bob got out of the car. A large golden dog hopped out after her.

Though as a rule Maddy liked cats better than dogs, she couldn't help staring at this one. He was so beautiful, and held his head so proudly . . . but somehow his brown eyes looked sad. *I wish I could play with him and cuddle him*, Maddy found herself thinking.

The woman clipped a lead onto the dog's collar and strode towards the front door. There was a rattling sound as the removals men slid the van door open. As Maddy watched, they started unloading furniture and boxes.

"We shouldn't stare," remembered Maddy's mother, dropping the curtain. "I dare say we'll meet her properly soon. It's a shame there don't seem to be any children for you and Jack to play with."

Maddy took a step backwards. "What kind of dog is that?" she asked, craning to see as the woman unlocked the door and went inside. The dog's feathery tail disappeared after her.

"A golden retriever," said Mum, settling down at the table again. "Pretty, isn't he? He certainly looks well-cared for, with that gorgeous coat."

Maddy nodded thoughtfully. She didn't really know much about dogs, she reminded herself. She'd probably been wrong to think that this one seemed sad. Maybe all golden retrievers looked like that.

Her father came out of his study and stretched. "Right, that's enough

work for a Saturday," he said. "You
too, Jenny. You've been studying for
hours. What do you say we have a
family game of something?"

Maddy's spirits leaped. "Yeah!" she
cried, doing a quick pirouette.

Mum laughed and closed her book.
"All right, twist my arm. Maddy, go
and get Jack, and we'll decide what to
play. Shall I make some nachos?"

The rest of the afternoon passed in
a happy blur of nachos and Cluedo.
Then, for dinner, they ordered in a
pizza and watched DVDs, so that
Maddy was feeling very stuffed and
content by the time she went upstairs
to get ready for bed.

Sleepily she started to get her
nightgown out of her chest of
drawers . . . and froze, staring at her

desk. One of the ceramic cats was missing! Only Greykin, the chunky grey cat, and Ollie, the long-haired tabby, were there. Where was Nibs, the slender black cat? Had she come to life?

Her heart thudding like a drum, Maddy glanced wildly around the room. "Nibs!" she hissed. "Nibs, where are you?"

For a moment nothing happened.
Then, with a *thump*, the tiny cat
appeared on the roof of the pink
plastic doll's house. "You certainly
took your time," she accused with
a sniff. "I thought you'd never get
here."

Relief washed over Maddy like a
bubbling stream. The magic *was* still
there after all. "Nibs!" she burst out,
hurrying over to the doll's house.
"You've come to life again – you
really have!"

The cat tried to look grumpy, but
Maddy could tell she was
holding back a smile.
"Well, of course," she
said.

"*May* I?" asked Maddy,
holding out her hand.

11

When she'd first met Nibs, she'd made the mistake of trying to stroke her too quickly, before the tiny cat was used to her. Though the two were good friends now, Maddy still thought she'd better ask.

Nibs pretended to be very busy washing her face. Finally she looked up and winked a bright green eye. "Oh, I suppose," she yawned. Suddenly leaping onto Maddy's palm, she rubbed against her fingers, purring.

"It's so good to see you!" exclaimed Maddy. She cuddled Nibs against her cheek, feeling her small, muscular softness. The little cat tilted her head back, and Maddy scratched under her chin with a fingernail.

"Mmm, yes, just there," sighed

Nibs contentedly.

There was a lot to catch up on, and soon the two were settled on the bed, chatting away. "Do you know why you're here?" asked Maddy.

Nibs shook her head. "No, my whiskers haven't tingled yet. I'll have a prowl around tonight and see what I can find out." She glanced at the window, her eyes gleaming.

Maddy smiled, remembering how much Nibs loved her night-time excursions.

"Greykin said the problem's going to be especially interesting this time," she commented. "I wonder what it'll be?"

Nibs glanced sharply at her. "He said what?"

Maddy repeated the words. To her surprise, Nibs didn't seem happy to hear this. Leaping off Maddy's arm onto the bedside table, she frowned across the room at the ceramic Greykin, swishing her tail back and forth.

Maddy knelt up. "Nibs? What is it?"

The tiny cat shook herself. "Nothing, I hope," she said grimly. "It's just that Greykin has a strange sense of humour sometimes."

"Oh," said Maddy. She looked
at the other two cats. Was it her
imagination, or did Greykin's smile
seem a little broader than usual?

"Well, never mind," said Nibs.
"We'll find out soon enough, I
suppose." Jumping back onto the
bed, she padded across the duvet
until she came to
the window. She
paused, gazing
upwards.

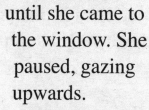

Realizing what
she wanted, Maddy
picked her up and
placed her on the
sill, and then slid
the window open a
crack. Cool spring air

swept into the room.

Nibs's eyes shone when she smelled the rich, earthy scent. "Lovely! I'll be back later."

Maddy tried not to feel disappointed that she was leaving so soon. Nibs wouldn't be Nibs without her night-time prowls. "I'll have your bed ready for you," she promised. This was a sock placed on the plastic doll's house bed, where Nibs slept curled up like

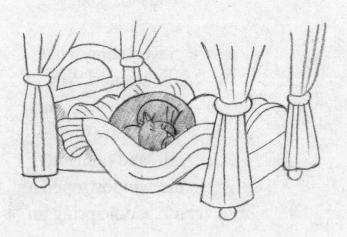

a tiny panther.

"Thanks." Giving Maddy's finger an affectionate nudge with her nose, Nibs slipped away into the night. Maddy watched her for as long as she could, but within seconds the little cat's black fur had merged with the shadows.

Maddy started as she heard a knock at her door. "Are you getting ready for bed in there?" called her mother.

"Yes," said Maddy quickly. She grinned as she went over to the chest of drawers again to get her nightgown. What had started out as a boring Saturday had now become absolutely wonderful!

I wonder what Greykin meant, though? she mused as she went into the bathroom to brush her teeth. Was

Nibs right? Was there something about this adventure that the grey cat found amusing?

Maddy didn't know . . . but she could hardly wait to find out!

First, though, they had to locate the problem. "It's not in the house," announced Nibs the next morning. She was sitting on her doll's house bed, giving herself a thorough wash.

Maddy knew better than to ask whether Nibs wanted anything to eat. The little cat hunted for her food herself, though Maddy preferred not to think about what it was she found!

"Maybe it's at school," she said, kneeling beside the doll's house. She felt a tickle of excitement at the thought. She loved taking the cats to school with her in her pencil case, and having a magical secret that the other pupils didn't know about.

Nibs paused in her washing, cocking her head to one side as if listening to something. "No, I don't think so," she said finally. "I feel like it's close by . . . it's just not *here*."

Maddy twirled a lock of hair around her finger, thinking hard. "Maybe it's one of the neighbours, then," she suggested. "We've got a new one – a woman moved in next door to us yesterday. She had a really pretty dog with her. Mum said it was a golden retriever, and it—"

She stopped abruptly. Nibs had stopped washing, and was staring at her. "A *dog*?" she echoed, her voice dripping with distaste.

Maddy nodded, wondering if she'd said something wrong. "What is it?"

The little cat sat staring across at Greykin, her green eyes narrowed. "Come on," she said suddenly, hopping down to the doll's house floor. "I really hope I'm wrong . . . but I have an awful feeling that we need to go and meet this new neighbour of yours!"

Chapter Two

Maddy glanced nervously over her shoulder as she went next door. To her relief, no one in her house was watching. Her mother thought she was playing in the meadow behind their back garden; she wouldn't be at all pleased if she knew what Maddy was up to. She'd almost certainly tell her not to bother their new neighbour.

Going up to the front door, Maddy took a deep breath and rang the bell.

Chapter Two

Panic struck her as she heard footsteps approach. "What should I say?" she whispered to Nibs. The little cat was sitting on her shoulder, hidden by her long hair.

Nibs shrugged. "How should I know? Welcome her to the neighbourhood, or something. You humans are good at small talk, aren't you?"

Maddy scowled down at her, thinking that this wasn't very helpful. Then she jerked up straight as the front door swung open. The woman she'd seen yesterday stood in the doorway, frowning.

"Yes?" she said shortly. Her silvery blonde bob looked as if it was sprayed into place, with every strand perfect.

Maddy put on a friendly smile. "Hi. I'm Maddy. I live next door." She pointed at her house.

The woman glanced at Maddy's house, and then back at her. "*Yes?*" she repeated, sounding impatient.

Maddy swallowed. She could feel Nibs listening tensely, her tiny tail twitching. "Well, I just wanted to say hello," she said. "Hello and . . . welcome to the neighbourhood."

The woman smiled, but it wasn't a very nice smile, thought Maddy – more of a grimace. "Thank you, how sweet," she said. "Well, if you'll excuse me, I've got a lot of unpacking to do." She started to close the door.

"No, wait!" burst out Maddy. She wasn't sure how much time Nibs needed to see if the problem was here, but thought she'd better keep the woman talking as long as possible. "Um – what's your name?"

The woman gave an irritated sigh. "Claire Flint. That's *Ms* Flint. Now, I really must be going . . ."

Suddenly Maddy spotted the golden retriever padding into the hallway behind Ms Flint. So did Nibs, who gave a startled hiss and gouged her claws into Maddy's shoulder.

"*Ow!*" she cried. Ms Flint gaped at her. "I mean – I mean, *wow*, you've got a dog," said Maddy weakly.

Up close, the retriever was even more attractive than he'd looked through their window. His golden coat was fluffy and gleaming, and there was a shiny leather collar around his neck. Though his brown eyes still looked sad, he seemed to smile as he gazed at Maddy, wagging his feathery tail.

"Go on, Star," said Ms Flint, turning to shoo the dog away. She glanced crossly back at Maddy.

"Look, it was nice to meet you, but I *really* must be going now." And with that, she banged the door shut in Maddy's face.

Back in her bedroom, Maddy rubbed her shoulder. "You didn't have to claw me," she complained. "That really hurt!"

Nibs didn't reply. She was prowling about on Maddy's desk, her slim black tail whipping back and forth like a snake. "I knew it," she muttered. "I just *knew* it!"

"Knew what?" asked Maddy. She sank into her chair.

Nibs stopped pacing and glared at the ceramic Greykin. "It's the dog, of course," she snapped. "That's what *he* thought was so funny. Yes – ha, ha.

Hilarious!"

Maddy blinked. "You mean, *Star* is the problem?"

Nibs scowled. "Imagine, *me* helping a dog!" she huffed. "It goes against every law of nature."

"But . . . what's wrong with him?" asked Maddy.

The cat hopped onto Maddy's mobile phone and tucked her paws under her body. "I don't know yet," she said sulkily. "I'll have to get closer to him to find out. *Ugh*." She shuddered in distaste.

"He looked really sad," said Maddy. A pang of worry went through her as she thought of the beautiful dog, and the unhappy expression in his eyes. "Oh, Nibs! Do you think he's OK?"

Nibs stared at her as if she were

mad. "Of course he's not OK," she said. "He's a *dog*. A big, clumsy, drooling, simple-minded—" She broke off, shaking her head. "Well, I suppose we'd better think of a plan," she muttered. "We have to get into that house so I can find out what the smelly brute's problem is."

"You mean – we'll have to *sneak* in?" Maddy frowned uncertainly. Though she wanted to help Star, this didn't sound quite honest, somehow. In fact, it sounded like something that her father had told her was called *trespassing*.

Nibs gave her an impatient look. "Well, I doubt if that woman would *invite* us in, don't you?"

Maddy knew she was right. "Yes, but – you just need to get close to

Star, right? We could wait until she's taking him for a walk or something, and . . ." She trailed off. The little cat was shaking her head.

"No, I might not have time. Inside the house is the best way." She gazed blankly at Maddy. "Is this one of those human moral things? We cats sneak about all the time, you know."

"All right," said Maddy reluctantly. At least she'd have her shadowy powers, she assured herself. Each of the cats could give Maddy a special magical power. With Nibs, Maddy could go *shadowy*, which was practically like being invisible. So far, though, she'd only tried it either in public or at home. The thought of going into someone else's house felt very different. What if Star started barking, and Ms Flint realized something was wrong?

Maddy pushed the idea away. "We'll need some help," she said, thinking aloud. "Because if I just ring her doorbell, then she'll open the door, think that no one's there, and close it again. I won't have time to slip past her."

Nibs twitched her ears. "A distraction," she agreed.

"Rachel!" burst out Maddy, bouncing on her seat. "She'd love to help, I know she would!" Her best friend had taken part in almost all the adventures with the cats so far, and was very good at thinking up plans.

Nibs made a face. "The nosy one?"

"She's not *nosy*," protested Maddy. "She's just . . . very scientific, that's all. She really wants to know where the three of you came from, and why." Maddy looked at the tiny cat hopefully. She hardly knew anything about the ceramic trio either, except that she'd got them at an antique fair in London.

"Mm," said Nibs, sounding bored. "Well, all right, I suppose she can help."

Maddy hesitated. "Nibs, where *did*—?" She stopped. The cat's green eyes were staring coolly at her, giving away nothing. "Never mind," she sighed, getting to her feet. "I'll go and ask Mum if Rachel can come over."

Lucky Star

* * *

Both their mothers agreed, and Rachel's mum dropped her off after lunch. "I can hardly wait to see Nibs again!" she whispered excitedly as they went upstairs. She was as tall as Maddy was short, with long blonde hair pulled back in a ponytail.

Maddy nodded. "But don't ask her any questions about where the cats came from, OK, Rache? She, um . . . doesn't want to talk about it."

At first Rachel looked as if she was about to argue, but then she sighed. "All right. My research can wait, I guess."

When they went into Maddy's bedroom, Nibs was sitting waiting for them on the doll's house chimney. Rachel's face lit up. "Hi, Nibs," she

said, going over to her. "Um . . . may I?" she asked, holding out her hand respectfully.

Maddy held her breath as Nibs gazed at Rachel. Finally the tiny cat yawned, showing rows of tiny white teeth. "Yes, all right."

Beaming, Rachel scratched Nibs's head with a single fingernail. Maddy knew just how she felt. Nibs took her time to get to know people, but when you were finally allowed to be her friend, you felt as if you'd won the lottery!

The two girls settled down on the floor beside the doll's house. Quickly Maddy explained what had happened. Rachel adjusted her glasses. "The problem is something to do with the *dog*?" she repeated in amazement.

Nibs winced. "Yes, I was surprised too," she muttered, looking away.

"And now I need to get into the house while I'm shadowy, so that Nibs can find out what's wrong," said Maddy. "Could you ring the doorbell and distract Ms Flint? You'll have to get her away from the door, somehow."

Rachel nodded, tapping her chin in thought. "It shouldn't be *too* hard."

Half an hour later, the three of them had worked out a plan. "Good," said Nibs briskly. "Let's go." She leaped down from the chimney onto the pink doll's house roof, where Maddy had stuck bits of Blu-Tack so that she didn't slip.

Maddy's throat went dry. "What – *now*? But – don't I need to practise going shadowy first?"

Nibs stared at her in surprise. "What for?"

"Well . . . just in case," faltered Maddy. It had been months since she'd gone shadowy, and it was an effort to stay invisible. What if she popped back into view in front of Ms Flint? The thought was too horrible to contemplate.

"You'll be fine," Nibs assured her. "You don't lose the skills once you have them. Here – see?"

As she spoke, Maddy felt a prickling sweep through her like

electricity, and then all at once she simply *faded*. She started, and stared down at herself in fascination. She'd forgotten how strange this was. She could see the doll's house through her arm!

"Maddy, that is *so* freaky," said Rachel in a hushed voice. She got up and circled her friend slowly, staring at her from every angle. "If I didn't know you were sitting right there . . ." She trailed off, shaking her head.

Nibs had gone shadowy too: a ghost cat sitting on the doll's house. As Maddy watched, she reappeared. Glancing down, Maddy realized that she had also become visible again.

"Now you," instructed Nibs.

To her relief, Nibs was right – remembering how to handle the magic

came back as easily as riding a bike. Concentrating, Maddy went shadowy again, and then brought herself back. The feline power flowed strongly through her, making her senses tingle.

"Hey, I did it!" She grinned.

Nibs rolled her eyes. "Well, of course," she said mildly. With a sudden leap, she flew from the doll's house roof and landed on Maddy's shoulder. "Now, come on. We've got a date with Fido!"

Chapter Three

"**M**um, we're going to go and play in the garden," called Maddy as she and Rachel went out of the back door. Nibs rode on her shoulder as usual, hidden by her hair.

Jack was down in the meadow, kicking a football around with some of the neighbourhood boys. "Ha!" she heard him shout. "I am the champion!"

Unnoticed, Maddy and Rachel slipped out of the back garden through the gate by the drive. After making sure no one was watching, Maddy summoned her cat magic. A moment later, she and Nibs had gone shadowy.

"This is really weird," said Rachel as they crossed over to Ms Flint's house. "Like being on my own, only I'm not."

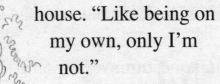

They went up to the door. "Good luck!" whispered Maddy, squeezing Rachel's arm. Then she hastily stood back as her friend rang the bell.

The door flew open even faster than it had the day before. Ms Flint stared down at

Rachel, not looking pleased to see another child on her doorstep. "Yes?" she said.

Rachel took a deep breath. "Um, hi," she said. "I just wanted to ask you . . . is that your car?" She pointed at the sleek black car in the drive.

Ms Flint frowned as if it were a trick question. "Why do you want to know?"

Rachel's eyes were wide and innocent. "Well, it's just that if it is, I thought I saw some boys doing something to one of the tyres."

Ms Flint's expression became thunderous. "Doing something to one of my *tyres*?" she spluttered.

Rachel nodded hard. "I don't know what, exactly. Maybe letting the air out, or—"

With a furious yelp, Ms Flint pushed past her and hurried over to the car. Maddy leaped backwards as she barrelled by without seeing her. "Where? Which one?" she demanded.

Rachel followed close behind. "This one," she said, pointing to the tyre that was furthest from the front door. "It was only a few minutes ago, so maybe it won't be deflating *just* yet . . ."

Well done, Rache! thought Maddy fervently. Without waiting to hear Ms Flint's response, she darted invisibly through the front door.

"Oh, yuck, do you smell that?" complained Nibs from her shoulder, screwing up her barely visible nose. "*Dog*. Pe-ew!"

It did smell a bit doggy in the house,

but Maddy didn't find it unpleasant.
Hurrying along the front hallway, she
came to what she guessed was the
lounge door. Taking a deep breath, she
eased it open and peered in.

The room was filled with half-
unpacked cardboard boxes. Star lay
curled up on a large red cushion,
gazing morosely at a TV in the corner.
On the shelf above him there was a

row of shiny gold and silver trophies. BEST IN SHOW, read one.

At the sound of the door Star looked up, thumping his tail – and then he stopped, gazing in confusion at the empty doorway.

Maddy hesitated, wondering what to do. Though he seemed a very nice dog, she wasn't at all sure how he'd react to invisible footsteps heading towards him! Perhaps she should become visible first? But before she could decide, Nibs padded down her arm to her hand.

"Right, this is the fun part," she said, gazing at Star in distaste. "Where I actually have to *talk* to the beast."

Maddy's jaw dropped. "Can you do that?" she whispered.

At the sound of voices Star leaped to his feet, staring wildly in all directions. *Woof!* he barked. *Woof, woof!*

Maddy glanced out of the window. Ms Flint was still bent over her tyre. Beside her, Rachel was talking earnestly, pointing at something. Deciding to take a chance, Maddy became visible again. The dog's eyes bulged, and he gave an uncertain whine.

"It's all right, Star, we're friends!" whispered Maddy. Seeing his tail begin to wag, she went over and scratched behind his floppy ears. "Good boy! We're friends," she repeated with a grin.

"Speak for yourself," grumbled Nibs. "OK, put me down, please. *Not* on that manky pillow."

Carefully Maddy placed the still-invisible Nibs on the carpet beside the cushion. The tiny cat flickered into view, and Star gave a surprised *woof*. Tail still wagging, he moved forward to sniff her.

With a hiss, Nibs arched her back like a Halloween cat. "Back, dog!" she spat, showing a paw full of claws. Star scrambled away in alarm.

"That's better," said Nibs darkly, returning to normal. "Honestly! No respect, dogs. Right, let's get this over with." Scowling, she went to the edge of the pillow and said something in a low voice. Star lay down with his nose on his paws, careful to keep his distance as he *woofed* softly back.

Maddy watched in amazement. The two of them were communicating! But what were they saying?

The animals murmured together for several minutes. Maddy sank back onto her haunches and stared, wishing she could understand what was being said. Suddenly she started as she heard the front door bang shut. Oh, no! Ms Flint was back!

Hurriedly Maddy summoned her feline magic and became invisible again just as Ms Flint came striding into the room. To Maddy's relief, she saw that Nibs had vanished as well. Star sat gazing around in bewilderment. After a moment he seemed to give up and looked at his mistress, his tail wagging hopefully.

All at once Maddy felt the tiny cat climbing up her jeans. A few seconds later she'd hopped onto her shoulder. "Ugh," she whispered, her whiskers tickling Maddy's ear. "Did you smell that creature's *breath*?"

Holding back a nervous giggle, Maddy started edging towards the door. Ms Flint was unpacking more trophies, grumbling to herself. "Silly little girl, wasting my time . . . her idea of a joke, I suppose, but it's not very funny . . ."

Leaving his cushion, Star nudged against her trouser leg, staring up at her with big brown eyes. "Yes, yes," she said impatiently, not looking at him. "Go and lie down now, Star. We'll go walkies later."

With a heavy sigh, the dog trudged back to his cushion and lay down again, gazing up at Ms Flint. Maddy paused. Poor Star! He seemed so unhappy. Well, hopefully Nibs knew what was wrong now, and they'd be able to help him.

Then Maddy gulped as something occurred to her. Slipping into the front hallway, she stared in dismay at the closed door. "Nibs, how am I going to get out?" she whispered.

"What do you mean?" the cat murmured back. "Just go out of the door. She can't see you."

"Yes, but she'll think she's going mad!" protested Maddy softly.

Nibs shrugged. "And?"

Maddy began to smile as she saw what Nibs meant. Even so, she tried to be quiet as she eased open the front door and stepped outside. But it was impossible to close it silently, and a moment later she heard Ms Flint's hurrying footsteps and a shout of: "Who's there?"

Without thinking, Maddy started running towards her own house. When she looked back, Ms Flint was standing on her doorstep, gazing up and down the street in confusion.

Grinning, Maddy slipped invisibly back through her garden gate.

As agreed, Rachel was waiting for her beside the fence. "Maddy, is that you?" she whispered nervously at the sound of footsteps.

By way of an answer, Maddy popped back into view only inches away. Rachel stifled a shriek, and then shoved her with a laugh. "Don't *do* that. You nearly gave me a heart attack." She grabbed Maddy's arm. "Come on – tell me everything!"

Stopping only to get a snack from the kitchen, the two girls hurried back to Maddy's bedroom. Nibs leaped up onto her doll's house bed. "I still smell of *dog*," she complained, her voice muffled as she attacked herself with her tongue. "Ick, ick, ick!"

"But, Nibs, what did you find out?" asked Maddy urgently. "She talked to Star for ages," she told Rachel.

"Really?" Rachel's eyes widened. "Is talking to dogs something all three of you can do? Where did you learn to—?" She broke off as Nibs paused in her washing to give her a look. "Sorry," she mumbled, her ears reddening.

"Nibs, *tell* us," said Maddy again.

Finally the little cat had cleaned herself to her satisfaction, and she curled up on the blue sock that covered the tiny bed. "Well, the problem is that Fido is unhappy," she said.

"I knew it!" exclaimed Maddy. "I thought he looked sad the very first time I saw him."

"Why isn't he happy?" asked Rachel, nibbling a biscuit.

"He wants an owner who really loves him," said Nibs. "He says that Ms Flint only cares about the trophies he wins at dog shows."

Lucky Star

Maddy thought of the row of gleaming cups, and of the way Ms Flint had ignored Star when he tried to get her attention. "Oh, the poor thing!" she breathed.

"Mm. It *is* a bit sad," admitted Nibs. "He was with a family once, and the children loved him, but then the parents decided that a dog was too much trouble and took him back to the breeder. So he was thrilled when Ms Flint bought him, but apart from training him for shows, she doesn't pay any attention to him. He says he'd give anything if she did."

Maddy felt as if her heart was breaking for the beautiful dog with the unhappy eyes. "We have to help him," she said, more to herself than the others. "We *have* to."

Rachel looked as worried as Maddy felt. "I don't know how," she said, shaking her head. "We can't *make* Ms Flint love Star."

"Well, frankly, I've never understood how *anyone* could care for a dog," observed Nibs. "But I agree that we have to help him. The question is . . . how?"

Maddy munched a biscuit gloomily as she thought. She and the cats had solved several problems together, but none had seemed as sad to her as this one. How could Ms Flint not care about a lovely dog like Star? It seemed impossible. And maybe, thought Maddy, that was the answer.

"I think – I think she *must* love him really," she said slowly. "Only maybe she doesn't realize it. But if we can somehow make her see how much she cares . . ."

Rachel's face lit up. "Maddy, that's a brilliant idea!" she cried. "You can do things that show her what a great dog Star is – how affectionate and gentle – and all sorts!"

Nibs's eyes narrowed in thought. "You know, that just might work," she said. "Good thinking, Maddy."

Maddy felt a warm glow at the praise. Nibs wasn't a cat who said something she didn't mean. She must really think it was a good idea.

"Here, let's make a list of all the things you can do!" exclaimed Rachel, finding a sheet of paper and a pen on Maddy's desk.

As the two girls started to plan, Maddy's spirits lifted still higher.

Lucky Star

Don't worry, Star, we're going to help you, she thought firmly. Her idea would work, she was sure of it.

Wouldn't it?

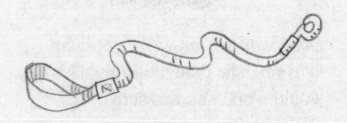

Chapter Four

"Hi, Ms Flint," called Maddy, running to catch up with her.

It was after school on Wednesday, and Ms Flint was striding across the meadow towards the copse, with Star trotting along beside her on his lead. As usual, his golden coat was fluffy and gleaming, though he looked as sad as ever.

"Hello," said Ms Flint without looking at Maddy. She didn't slow down, so that Maddy had to jog to keep up.

Though her neighbour didn't seem in the mood to talk, Maddy didn't dare let this opportunity go by. She'd been watching out for Ms Flint and Star for days now, and this was the first time she'd spotted them.

"That's a golden retriever, isn't it?" she asked breathlessly, skipping backwards to face Ms Flint.

Her neighbour frowned, and went round her. "Yes, he is."

"Can I pet him?" asked Maddy. Star wagged his tail hopefully.

"I'm afraid not." Ms Flint walked even faster.

Maddy put on a burst of speed to keep up. "You know, I've been reading about golden retrievers," she said. "They're very intelligent dogs, aren't they? And really loyal, and playful, and—"

"*Playful?*" Ms Flint stopped in her tracks, staring coldly at Maddy. "Star doesn't *play*. He's a highly valuable show dog, and he needs a very particular routine."

Star gazed up at her as she spoke, his brown eyes pleading with her. Though Maddy had hardly spent any time around dogs before, it was obvious to her what he was saying: *Please, please love me! I don't care about being a show dog!*

"He, um . . . seems sort of sad," ventured Maddy.

"Nonsense," snapped Ms Flint, striding off again. "What would he have to be sad about? He's a perfectly trained dog – he won Best in Show at Westchester just last month."

"But – but maybe he wants to play, and have fun – and—" *And know that you love him*, Maddy almost said.

She didn't have a chance. "Little girl, I really must be going now," interrupted Ms Flint with a glare. "Run along home, will you?" And she headed off into the copse, with Star trotting miserably at her side.

"Maddy," whispered Maddy to herself, staring after them. "My name's Maddy." Shivering suddenly in her jacket, she turned and trudged sadly home.

That night Maddy picked at her dinner, thoughts of Star whirling around in her head. The first item on her and Rachel's list had been: *Talk to Ms Flint about how wonderful golden retrievers are!* – but that hadn't gone down very well, had it? What if her idea didn't work after all?

"Maddy, is everything OK?" asked Dad.

"Mm?" Maddy looked up. "Yes, I'm just – just thinking."

"Don't think too hard, your brain might explode," sniggered Jack. Maddy made a face at him.

"Eat your peas, Jack," said Mum. "Maddy, actually I wanted to ask you something. You know the village fete is coming up next weekend?"

"Is it?" said Maddy, still thinking about Star.

Mum nodded. She had brown hair like Maddy's, but hers was shoulder-length, and she was always scraping it quickly back with one hand. "Yes, it is. And I told Mrs Anderson that I'd run the stall for the Heart Fund. Would you like to help?"

"Hey! Why can't *I* help?" protested Jack loudly.

"You can if you want to." Mum shrugged. "I just thought it would be

more Maddy's thing. You'd have to
stay at the stall for hours, you know,
selling things for charity."

"Yes, so no messing about if you
do it," said Dad. "*Peas*, Jack." He
pointed his fork at Jack's plate.

"Oh." Jack played with his peas,
considering. "No, I don't think I will,"
he decided.

Mum hid a smile. "Maddy, how
about you?"

Maddy had only been half listening.
"Yes, OK," she agreed.

"Great!" said Mum, beaming.
"We'll have a lot of fun, and it's for a
really good cause. I've heard that our
new neighbour will be at the fete as
well," she added.

Maddy looked up quickly. "She will?"

"Yes, there's going to be a dog

show for all the local dogs," Mum explained, helping herself to more chicken. "Ms Flint is going to do a special demonstration with Star, and show everyone a few training techniques. Apparently she's planning on starting up a dog obedience school here, so she wants to show off what he can do."

"I wish there were *child* obedience schools," teased Dad. "I'd send you two off in a flash."

Jack dissolved into giggles. "Woof, woof!" he barked. "Woof, woof!"

Maddy was quiet, thinking about what Mum had just said. Wouldn't it be wonderful if by the time the fete came round, Ms Flint had realized how much she cared for Star?

She crossed her fingers tightly under

the table. *Please*, she thought. *Please let it happen!* But somehow she had an awful feeling that it wasn't going to be as easy as they'd thought.

The second item on the list was: *Play with Star, and show Ms Flint how lovely he is!*

"It might take me ages, though," said Maddy to Rachel at school the next day as they sat on the swings at break. She dragged her toe along the ground, spinning herself sideways. "It was days before I managed to talk to her about golden retrievers. And a whole lot of good *that* did."

Rachel's blue eyes were sympathetic. "Just keep trying. It'll work, it *has* to!"

Maddy sighed, and pressed her

cheek against the cool chain. "I hope you're right."

"Me too," said Rachel glumly.

The two girls swung in silence for a moment. Suddenly Maddy's attention was caught by a Year Three girl with wavy black hair. She was playing cards with a few other girls, but she seemed unhappy to Maddy, as if she were thinking of something sad.

"Rachel, look at that girl —" she started, and then broke off as the bell rang. Everyone started drifting towards the school doors.

"What girl?" asked Rachel as they hopped off the swings and headed inside with the others.

Maddy looked again. The girl was walking a little ahead of them, but now she was smiling and laughing with her friends, as if nothing was wrong after all.

"Er – never mind," said Maddy, feeling a bit silly. *I must have imagined it*, she thought, shaking her head. Great. She was so worried about Star that she was seeing things!

When Maddy got home
from school, she saw
Nibs sitting on her
bedroom windowsill,
staring out at the back
garden. As always, a thrill
ran through Maddy at the
sight of the tiny cat. Though she'd had
the cats for months now, she knew
she'd never get tired of having such
amazing magic in her life.

"Oh, good, you're back," said Nibs,
glancing over her shoulder at Maddy.
"Come here – you have *got* to see
this."

Curious, Maddy crossed to the
window and looked out. "Oh!" she
exclaimed. In the next garden she
could see Ms Flint and Star. But *what*
were they doing?

Lucky Star

As she watched, Ms Flint sprinted about the garden in a large circle, with Star trotting on his lead beside her, matching her step for step. "Head up," Maddy heard her say. He lifted his head.

Maddy bit her lip. Star looked noble and beautiful . . . but he didn't seem to be enjoying himself. After a while

Ms Flint stopped. Taking Star off his lead, she strode all around the garden with him. He walked perfectly at heel, no matter how sharply she twisted and turned.

"Obedience training," sniffed Nibs. She shook her head. "Dogs really have no pride at all."

Down below, Ms Flint threw something that looked like a small dumbbell. Star sat waiting at her side, not moving. "Now!" Maddy heard faintly, and the dog galloped off, retrieving the dumbbell and bringing it smartly back.

Poor Star, thought Maddy. His mistress didn't so much as pat him on the head when he did something right!

Suddenly Ms Flint looked back towards her house. A moment later she was heading inside, leaving Star in the garden.

"Phone," said Nibs, whose hearing was sharper than Maddy's. With a small, muscular leap, she bounded onto Maddy's arm. "Come on! Remember number two on the list – this is our chance!"

Maddy's heart leaped as she realized Nibs was right. This was the perfect opportunity to play with Star, so that Ms Flint could see how lovely he was! Hurrying downstairs, she went out of the back door and over to the fence that divided the two gardens. Stepping onto a large rock in their flowerbed, she could see over it easily.

"Hi, Star!" she called, waving at the dog.

The golden retriever's face lit up. Bounding over, he stood on his hind legs so that Maddy could stroke him. She smiled as she fondled his floppy ears. They were so silky!

"I see that his breath hasn't improved any," sighed Nibs from her shoulder. "What about that ball on the ground?"

Glancing down, Maddy saw an old tennis ball and quickly grabbed it. "Look, Star!" she exclaimed, holding it up. "Do you want to play fetch?"

He barked excitedly, dancing about on the spot. Maddy threw the ball into his garden. "Fetch!" she cried. Star leaped after it. He was back at the fence in a moment, standing on his hind legs again and holding the ball in his mouth.

"Good boy," praised Maddy,
stroking his head and accepting the
somewhat soggy ball. "Here, let's
go again! Fetch!" She flung the ball

and Star dashed after it once more, bringing it back to her just as quickly. His brown eyes shone with fun.

Over and over Maddy threw the ball for the delighted dog. Finally it landed in a hedge and Star raced after it, diving head-first into the foliage. Maddy giggled as she watched his feathery tail wag. He was having the time of his life! Now all she needed was for Ms Flint to see him. Surely she'd realize what a fantastic dog he was then, apart from winning trophies.

"*What* is going on here?" demanded an angry voice.

"Uh-oh," muttered Nibs, retreating behind Maddy's long hair.

Maddy gulped. Ms Flint was back, but she didn't look at all pleased.

Instead, she was standing a few paces away with her hands on her hips.

"What are you doing up there?" she asked Maddy suspiciously.

"We've – we've been playing fetch," stammered Maddy. "Um . . . maybe you'd like to have a go?"

"*Fetch?*" echoed Ms Flint in horror. "But—" She broke off as Star suddenly burst out of the hedge and came bouncing over to her with the tennis ball in his mouth. He sat at her feet, his eyes sparkling. Again, Maddy knew just what he was thinking: *Come on, play with me! Let's have some fun!*

Ms Flint gazed down at her eager dog, and seemed to hesitate for a moment. Maddy felt tense with hope.

"Star really seemed to be enjoying it," she said shyly. "You should have seen him! His tail was wagging, and—"

With a grimace, Ms Flint grabbed the tennis ball from Star and marched across to Maddy. "Here," she snapped, handing it back. "Now, I must ask you to leave us alone. We're doing some very important training, and Star mustn't be disturbed. *Fetch* is not at all appropriate for champions like him!"

Lucky Star

Star's ears seemed to wilt further with every word. The light dimmed from his eyes as he lay down on the grass, resting his nose on his paws.

"But—" started Maddy.

"*Now*," said Ms Flint.

"All right," mumbled Maddy, her cheeks flushing. "I mean – um – sorry." She stepped down off the rock, and Ms Flint's back garden disappeared from view. A moment later, she heard the sound of Star's training starting up again.

"Don't feel bad," whispered Nibs, nuzzling against her ear. "We'll just have to try something else, that's all."

But as Maddy sat at her desk later and gazed glumly down at their list, she wasn't at all sure any more that any of their ideas would work. She couldn't see Ms Flint being impressed by a book on golden retrievers left on her doorstep, or by an invisible Maddy encouraging Star to rest his head on her knee. She'd probably just order him to go back to his cushion!

Maddy groaned in frustration. "I *know* she must really care about him, deep down," she said. "We just have to make her realize it! What we need is for Star to – to rescue her from a burning building, or dive into the water to save her, like dogs do in films!"

Nibs was sitting on the list, studying it along with Maddy. She looked up sharply. "Now, *that's* a thought."

"Hang on, I wasn't being serious," said Maddy in alarm. "We can't have Star rescue Ms Flint *really* – not without putting her in some kind of danger. And that probably wouldn't be a very good idea."

Nibs curled her slim black tail around a full stop. "True," she purred. "But *you* could be in danger, couldn't you?"

Maddy's eyebrows drew together in confusion. "I could?"

"Yes, or you could pretend to be," explained Nibs. "And then good old Fido could come along and rescue you. Who could resist such a lovable pooch as that?" She winked.

Maddy gasped as she suddenly saw what the little cat meant. "Nibs, you're a genius!" she exclaimed. "I think that'll work, I really do!"

Nibs smiled, and began to wash her inky black face. "Well, I do try," she said modestly.

Chapter Five

It was Sunday before Maddy saw Ms Flint and Star again. She'd spent the whole morning looking out for them, but it wasn't until just after lunch that she was rewarded by the sight of Ms Flint striding across the meadow, with Star on his lead. This was her chance!

"Mum, can I go out and play?" she asked, dashing into the lounge.

Her mother barely looked up from her textbook. "Yes, all right. Don't go beyond the meadow."

"I won't!" promised Maddy. She pounded upstairs to get Nibs, and then grabbed her jacket and raced outside, turning shadowy on the run.

Nibs stood on her shoulder, balancing herself with her tail. "That way," she said, nudging Maddy towards the copse. Maddy ran as fast as she could, and a moment later saw Ms Flint just ahead of her, following the path through the trees. Star ambled along at her side, his golden ears drooping.

Maddy frowned. This would be much easier out in the open! Still, there was no help for it. She crept along after Ms Flint and Star. If she could just get alongside them, then she could let Star off his lead as they'd planned . . .

Her foot snapped a twig. Both Star and Ms Flint looked round. Maddy froze, her heart beating hard.

Ms Flint stared at the empty path. "Strange . . ." she murmured. Suddenly there was a buzzing sound as her mobile went off. She reached into her pocket. "Oh, hello, Mum. Yes, just walking Star . . ."

Phew, thought Maddy. Very quietly, she crept forward again.

"That's right, next Saturday,"

Ms Flint went on. "I'm going to put Star through his paces . . . it should be great exposure for the new school . . ."

Maddy drew up alongside them, her invisible trainers sinking into the undergrowth. She crouched down beside Star. He gave an uneasy whine, his tail wagging uncertainly.

"Hang on, I'll have a word with him," murmured Nibs. Padding down Maddy's arm until she was level with the dog's ear, she said something in a low voice. Star sat very still, listening hard.

"OK, I think he gets it," hissed Nibs, returning to Maddy's shoulder.

Lucky Star

Maddy hoped the little cat was right. This could all go terribly wrong otherwise! As Ms Flint chatted away, Maddy invisibly stroked Star's head . . . and then let her hand slide down to his collar. Very carefully she unsnapped his lead, holding it in place so that it wouldn't drop to the ground just yet.

Just to make sure, she leaned down and whispered, "Star, will you come with me? Please? It's for a really good reason."

Star's brown eyes seemed to meet hers, though Maddy knew that was impossible given that he couldn't see her. Had the dog understood? Taking a deep breath, she grabbed his collar and let go of his lead. *Now!*

She dashed off, pulling Star along

with her. To her relief, the golden
retriever galloped readily at her side.
They pounded together down the
winding path, faster than Maddy had
ever run before.

"*Star!*" shouted Ms Flint behind
them. "Star, come back here! *STAR!*"

Hearing his mistress's command,
Star hesitated, looking back. Maddy
tugged frantically at his collar. "Not
yet!" she hissed.

Maddy felt Nibs leap off her arm
and, from Star's startled yelp, realized
that she'd landed squarely on the

dog's head. "Ignore her!" the little cat
yowled. "Come on, Star, this is for
your own good!"

Star seemed to make up his mind,
and ran faster than ever, with the
shadowy Nibs perched on his head
like a tiny jockey. Ms Flint came
crashing through the undergrowth
after them, shouting, "Star! *Star!*"
Maddy gulped. She was very glad that
she couldn't be seen!

Then all at once they'd left the
copse, and were in a field. Maddy
looked around frantically, and spied

a large fallen log near the trees.
Perfect! Making herself visible again,
she hastily lay down on the ground
beside it. Nibs hopped back onto her
shoulder, nestling under her collar.

"Sit, Star," panted Maddy. "Sit!"

Star sat down beside her just as
Ms Flint came staggering out of the
woods, her perfect hair dishevelled.
"*There* you are!" she exclaimed,
hurrying over. "Bad dog!" She clipped
the lead back onto his collar.

Star hung his head, looking
wretched. "But Ms Flint, he's not a
bad dog at all! He saved me!" cried
Maddy, propping herself up on her
elbows.

Ms Flint blinked as if she'd only
just noticed Maddy. "He *what*?"

"I – I was playing, and I somehow

got trapped under the log," said
Maddy, crossing her fingers against
her side. "I've been here for hours!
And then Star came running up,
just like he knew I was here, and he
dragged me out. He probably saved
my life!"

Ms Flint stared down at her dog.
"He did?"

"Yes!" cried Maddy, encouraged.
She sat up. "He's a hero, he really is.
You should be *so* proud of him!"

Ms Flint looked taken aback.
"Well, I —" She broke
off, studying
Maddy
closely.
"You've
been
there for

hours, you say?"

Maddy nodded hard.

Ms Flint glanced at the fallen log, and then back at Maddy. "Well, you look awfully clean to have been lying under a dirty log for hours. And I don't see any marks on the ground where Star might have dragged you out, either."

Maddy felt her cheeks turn bright red. "Er . . ."

"Star didn't save you at all, did he?" demanded Ms Flint.

"Um . . . well . . . he *would* have, if I'd needed him to," stammered Maddy. "He really is a lovely dog, Ms Flint – he's so sweet, and gentle, and—"

Ms Flint's eyes flashed. "Now, listen! I've had just about enough

of you interfering with my dog.
You are to *leave him alone*, do you
understand? He's a very expensive
show dog, and—"

"But he doesn't care about being a
show dog!" cried Maddy, leaping to
her feet. "He just wants you to love
him, that's all!"

"What do you mean?" spluttered Ms
Flint. "Of course he cares about being
a show dog! He always performs
beautifully – everyone says so—"

Maddy felt like stamping her foot.
"But he only does it to please you! He
needs love, not trophies!"

Ms Flint started to say
something and then
stopped. Maddy held
her breath in hope.
For a moment Ms Flint

looked uncertain. Then she shook
herself.

"I have had quite enough of this
conversation," she said coldly. She
tugged on Star's lead. "Come along,
Star. Heel!"

She started back into the copse
with Star at her side, his golden
head drooping sadly. Unable to stop
herself, Maddy darted after her,
tugging at her arm. She felt close to
tears. "Ms Flint, *please*! Can't you see
how unhappy he is? He needs to know
that you care about him—"

Ms Flint shook her off. "Leave me
alone, or I'll go and speak to your
mother! Star has a very important
exhibition next weekend. He *cannot*
have this sort of disruption."

Star gazed up at her, his brown

eyes melting.

"But don't you love him at all?" choked out Maddy. "Even just a little bit? He tries so hard for you—"

"He's a *dog*," snapped Ms Flint. "He does what he's told, and I wish you would too."

She disappeared into the wood with Star. Maddy stared after them, hot tears running down her face. Nibs crept out onto her shoulder. Standing on her hind legs, she patted Maddy's cheek gently with her paw. "Hey," she whispered. "Don't cry. You did your best."

Though Maddy knew she needed to get home, she found herself sinking onto the fallen log. "Oh, Nibs!" she sobbed. "She *doesn't* love Star. She really doesn't!"

Lucky Star

Nibs sighed. "I think you're right," she admitted. "Some people are like that, I suppose. Their pets are just *things* to them." She leaned against Maddy's damp cheek. Though Maddy couldn't stop crying, part of her felt a tiny bit better, just knowing that Nibs was there.

After a while she sniffed, and stroked Nibs's fur. She giggled despite herself. "Oh, Nibs . . . you're all wet!"

"Yes, well." Nibs smiled as she looked down ruefully. "It didn't seem quite the time to mention it."

Maddy dried Nibs off with her sleeve as best she could. "I suppose we'd better start for home," she said with a sigh. "Mum'll go mad if she sees we're not in the meadow."

As they trudged back through the copse, Maddy shoved her hands into her jacket pockets, feeling discouraged. "There's no way to solve the problem, then, is there?" she said. "She doesn't love him, and that's that."

Nibs sounded thoughtful. "There might be another way, though."

"Really?" Maddy peered at the little cat on her shoulder. "What?"

"Well, the problem is that Star wants to be with an owner who loves him," said Nibs with a shrug.

"Ms Flint doesn't . . . and so we'll just have to find him someone who does."

Maddy stopped short. "Of course!" she breathed. For a moment wonderful possibilities seemed to open up before her: Star with a family who really loved him, romping and playing together, sleeping curled up on his owner's bed . . .

Then reality came crashing in. "But, Nibs, *how*? He's her dog! Maybe she doesn't love him, but she doesn't want to give him up, either." Maddy started walking again, and came out into the meadow. To her relief, her mother was nowhere in sight.

"Oh, there are ways," said Nibs airily.

Maddy gave the cat a suspicious glance. "What ways? Nibs, we can't *steal* him. It would be wrong, and besides, he's probably got one of those chip things in him, so that—"

Nibs sounded insulted. "I wasn't thinking of *stealing* him. There's more than one way to skin a cat, you know. Excuse the vile expression."

"What, then?" asked Maddy. Climbing onto the gate that led into their garden, she swung gently on it.

In a small black blur, Nibs jumped down from her shoulder to her arm.

"Easy," she said, blinking her green eyes. "All she cares about is dog shows, right? So . . . what if Star did really, really badly at one?"

"Or at the village fete!" burst out Maddy, standing straight up on the gate. "Nibs, that's it! She's doing a special demonstration with Star at

the fete next weekend, so that people
will hire her to train their dogs. If
he doesn't behave at *that*, she'll be
furious!"

"Even better!" purred Nibs. "If
people think she can't even train her
own dog, then no one's going to hire
her – and she certainly won't want
Star any more."

Maddy hesitated as she remembered
how guilty and miserable Star had
looked just now. "But . . . how do we
get him to misbehave? I don't think
he's going to want to do anything
wrong again, after this."

"Oh, you can leave that part to me."
Nibs casually inspected one claw-
filled paw. "*You* just need to worry
about finding him a new home!"

Chapter Six

"**B**ut how can we find Star a new home?" protested Rachel at school the next day. "He's already *got* a home."

"Yes, but not for long," said Maddy. It was lunch time, and they were sitting in the school canteen eating sausages and chips. As usual, everyone was making such a noise that they could talk without being overheard.

"When Star misbehaves on

Saturday, Ms Flint is sure to want
to get rid of him," she explained.
"Maybe even there and then! So we
need to find him a new home, and
make sure that person's at the fete to
take him home with them." Maddy
couldn't help smiling at the thought of
Star having a new owner – someone
who really loved him.

Rachel rolled her eyes. "Yes, but
how?" she demanded. "We can't say
to people, 'Would you like a dog? Of
course, his owner doesn't know yet
that she's giving him away, but she's
sure to on Saturday.' We'd sound
mad!"

Maddy chewed her lip, her
happiness fading. Rachel was
right. This wasn't going to be easy.
"Um . . . I suppose we'll have to ask

people if they'd like a dog *in theory*.
You know – *if* they could have a dog,
would they? And then we'll make
sure they're at the fete, and just hope
for the best."

Rachel gave her a long look. "That
doesn't sound very scientific, Maddy."

"Well, we have to try," insisted
Maddy. "Star might end up in a
shelter otherwise! And I know *I* can't
have him. Jack's allergic to dog fur."
She gasped as a thought occurred
to her. "Hang on, could *you* take
him? Oh, Rachel! That would solve
everything!"

Rachel shook her head. "No, Mum
says dogs are too much trouble." She
sighed and started on her fruit salad.
"All right, I'll help. But if everyone
thinks we're mad, I'm blaming you!"

The two friends spent the rest of their lunch break planning. The best thing, they decided, was to pretend they were taking a pet survey. Then they could find out who in Year Five might be allowed to have a dog, and hopefully find a home for Star that way.

"Not Sherry, though," said Maddy, making a face. The class bully was much improved since Maddy had taught her a lesson with cat magic, but she still wasn't someone Maddy would want Star to live with!

"We'll have to include her if we're doing a survey," Rachel pointed out. She was already busy writing down a list of questions. "But don't worry, I don't think she'd be able to take Star anyway. Her family lives in a flat."

As the girls found out over the next few days, this was a common problem. The children they questioned either couldn't have a dog for some reason – though almost all of them wanted one – or else they already had a pet and their parents didn't want another.

By afternoon break on Friday, there were only two names left on Rachel's list. Maddy gazed down at them anxiously, feeling more worried than ever. She'd had a wonderful time with Nibs this week, but the fete was *tomorrow* – and they hadn't found a single possible home for Star yet!

"Here," said Rachel, handing her a copy of the survey. She had printed it off on her home computer, and it looked very professional. "You do Nathan. I'll go and talk to Freya. Good luck!"

Nathan was a stocky boy with a round face and freckles. Maddy found him playing on the jungle gym with his friend Ben. "Hi, Nathan," she called up to him. "Do you want to do our pet survey?"

Swinging himself off a bar, Nathan

dropped to the ground beside her. "OK," he said cheerfully.

Ben hooted down at them. "Ooh! Look who's got a girlfriend!"

Nathan rolled his eyes. "Ignore him," he said as they walked a few steps away. "He's really immature."

Maddy wrote Nathan's name at the top of the page. "All right, the first question is, *Do you have any pets?*" She held her pen over the paper, waiting.

He shook his head. "I had a goldfish once, but it died."

No, wrote Maddy neatly. "Would you like a pet?"

"Definitely!" exclaimed Nathan. "I love animals. I want to be a vet when I grow up."

Yes, definitely, wrote Maddy. "OK,

if you could have a pet, what sort of animal would it be?"

Nathan considered this. "For real, or pretend? Because if I could have *anything*, I'd have a wolf. Or maybe a leopard."

"No, for real," said Maddy.

"A dog, then," said Nathan promptly. "Dogs are great."

Maddy took a deep breath. It was the next question that had always turned out to be so disappointing. "All right . . . Would your parents let you have a pet?"

"Maybe," said Nathan. "They're always saying we'll get a dog someday."

Maddy almost dropped her pen. "*Really?*"

He nodded. "Yeah, they both love

dogs. The only reason we haven't got one is that both my parents work, and they say it's not fair to leave a dog alone all day. But now my mum's started her own business from home, so we could probably have one."

"Nathan! That's great!" gasped Maddy.

He stared at her. "It is? Why?"

Maddy caught herself. "I just mean

– it's great that you might get a dog soon. I love dogs too! Are you going to the village fete tomorrow?"

He blinked at the change of subject. "Is that one of the questions?"

"No, I'm just asking," said Maddy eagerly. "Because there's going to be a dog show, and I bet you'd really, really like it. Nathan, you *have* to go!"

"Oh." He shrugged in confusion. "I can't, though – we're going to Southampton this weekend, to visit my grandmother for her birthday."

No! Maddy almost shouted the word out loud. "But you *have* to come," she wailed. "Nathan, you just *have* to!"

Looking at her strangely, Nathan edged back towards the jungle gym. "Um . . . is that all the questions?"

"Are you really sure you can't

come?" asked Maddy in a tiny voice. "I mean – completely, absolutely sure?"

"Positive!" said Nathan. He swung himself quickly up the bars again. As Maddy turned to leave, she heard him say to Ben, "You've got a point about girls. They're pretty weird!"

Maddy was too upset to be bothered. She couldn't believe she'd been so close. Nathan's family would have been perfect for Star, just perfect!

From the expression on Rachel's face, Maddy knew that she hadn't had any better success with Freya. "She hates dogs," said Rachel gloomily as they met up at the side of the playground. "She thinks they're smelly."

"That's everyone, then," whispered Maddy. She slumped against the chain-link fence. "Oh, Rachel! What are we going to do?"

"It's only everyone in Five A and Five B," corrected Rachel. "But we don't have time now to ask the other years." She nibbled her thumb. "It doesn't *have* to be tomorrow, does it? Couldn't Nibs make Star misbehave at one of his important dog shows instead?" Her face lit up. "Yes! You could turn invisible, and sneak along in the car with Ms Flint—"

"But how would we know when it is?" protested Maddy. "And even if we knew, how could we make sure that someone's there who wants to give Star a home? It has to be the fete, it just *has* to!"

Rachel's face was pinched with worry. "How can we find someone by tomorrow, though? We can't just start asking people randomly—"

"Wait a minute," interrupted Maddy, straightening up from the fence. She'd just spotted the Year Three girl with dark wavy hair – the one who she'd thought had seemed sad the week before. She was sitting on a bench by herself,  drawing something in a notebook.

Maddy stared at her. She knew that sometimes the cats' whiskers tingled, telling them important things.

She herself didn't have whiskers, of course . . . but right now she was tingling nonetheless.

She quickly turned to Rachel. "Do you have another survey sheet?"

Rachel pulled one out of her folder. "Here – but who are you going to ask?"

"Her," said Maddy, pointing. "I've just . . . got a funny feeling, that's all."

Rachel looked sceptical. "Well, I hope your funny feeling's right."

Me too, thought Maddy as she crossed the playground. The dark-haired girl glanced up as Maddy approached her, and quickly closed her notebook.

"Um, hi," said Maddy, sitting next to her. "I'm Maddy. You're in Year Three, aren't you? What's your name?"

"Sophie," said the girl shyly. She was very pretty, but Maddy realized she'd been right: Sophie *was* sad. She could practically feel it coming off her in great waves.

"My friend and I are doing a pet survey," said Maddy. "Would you like to take it?"

Sophie seemed to shrink at the word "pet". "I suppose," she mumbled.

Maddy hesitated, thinking that maybe she should just leave Sophie alone . . . but then she thought of Star and forced herself. She wrote Sophie's name on the paper. "Right, the first question is . . . Do you have a pet?"

"No," said Sophie softly. "We had a dog, but . . . he died a few months ago."

"I'm sorry," said Maddy, stricken. No wonder Sophie was so sad! "What – what happened to him?"

Sophie made a face, and Maddy knew she was trying not to cry. "He was hit by a car. He was a chocolate lab called Truffles, and – and he was the best dog in the world. Here, look." Opening her notebook, she showed Maddy her drawing: a big, smiling dog playing with a dark-haired girl. *Me and Truffles* was written above.

Sophie wiped her sleeve across her eyes. "I've really been missing him a lot lately," she choked out. "It's my birthday on Sunday, and that's when we first got him, for my birthday two years ago . . ." She trailed off.

Excitement flickered through Maddy. It was awful that Sophie was so unhappy, but maybe, just maybe . . . Glancing down at her survey, she skipped ahead a few questions. "Um, Sophie . . . do you think your parents would let you have another dog?"

"Yes, they want me to," admitted Sophie, tracing a finger over her drawing. "They know how much I miss Truffles, but – but I don't know. Another dog wouldn't be the same."

"No, but he might be just as nice in a different way," Maddy pointed out, her heart pounding. The tingling had been right! Sophie was the perfect person for Star. The two of them *needed* each other. "Sophie, listen," she said urgently. "Is your family coming to the village fete tomorrow?"

The smaller girl looked startled. "Well – I *think* so. We usually do."

"Oh, *please* do," said Maddy. "I can't tell you everything, but – but there's a dog at the dog show that needs a home, and I think he'll be just right for you. But you have to be there!"

Sophie's eyes widened. "A dog? But—"

"He's perfect for you," repeated Maddy firmly. "And you're perfect for him. Promise you'll be there, OK?"

Sophie hesitated. There was an odd expression on her face – half hopeful and half reluctant. For a long moment she gazed down at her drawing, and then she slowly closed her notebook.

"OK," she agreed. "We'll come to the dog show. And Maddy . . . is he a *nice* dog?"

"The nicest dog in the world!" Maddy assured her with a grin. "You're going to love him, I promise!"

She was practically dancing as she went back to Rachel. Her best friend stared at her eagerly. "What? What?" she exclaimed, grabbing Maddy's arm.

"Oh, Rachel!" gasped Maddy as the bell rang. "Just wait till I tell you – I think I've found a home for Star after all!"

Chapter Seven

The next day dawned bright and sunny. "*That's* a relief," said Maddy's mum cheerfully as she and Maddy set up their stall at the fete. "I'd hate to be standing out here in the rain all day."

Maddy nodded, but her mind was on the ring that was being prepared for the dog show later, behind the food stalls. In fact, the whole village green was being transformed, with tents and games everywhere.

The stall that Maddy and her mother were running was filled with items from the Heart Fund's charity shop – old clothes, CDs, books, and lots of things that Maddy couldn't put a name to at all.

"Unusual taste, some people!" giggled Mum, unpacking a bright pink ceramic shepherdess with billowing skirts. "Maddy, wouldn't this look nice beside your ceramic cats? She could herd them for you."

"Good idea," said Maddy, managing a grin. On her shoulder, she heard Nibs give a tiny, disdainful sniff.

Maddy glanced in the direction of the ring again. The dog show began at one o'clock. How was she going to get away, when Mum expected her to help? *I'll just have to manage it*

somehow, she told herself.

At ten o'clock the fete opened and people started to arrive. Maddy kept a close eye out for Sophie and her family, but didn't see them anywhere. She gazed worriedly around at the crowd. What if Sophie had decided not to come?

Nibs was lying quietly on her shoulder, hidden by Maddy's long hair. Suddenly she sat up and whispered, "A dog's coming. I think it's Star."

Sure enough, Ms Flint had appeared on the green with Star on his lead. The two of them walked grandly past the stalls. But Star's brown eyes were wells of misery, and Maddy swallowed hard. He looked even sadder now than before! If their plan

didn't work . . .

Not wanting Ms Flint to recognize her, Maddy quickly busied herself with some CDs as they passed. *Star, don't worry!* she thought fervently. *After today, everything will be OK, I promise!*

Mum had been watching them as well. "Odd woman," she murmured to herself.

Maddy glanced up in surprise. "Do you mean Ms Flint? Why?"

Mum looked as if she wished she hadn't said anything. "Nothing. It's just that I met her in the village shop a few days ago, and . . . well, she didn't seem very happy, that's all."

Maddy was startled. "But she has all her dog show trophies. Don't *they* make her happy?" Then she wanted to pop her hand over her mouth. What if Mum asked how she knew?

Lucky Star

Luckily her mother didn't seem to notice. "Mm, that's what I mean," she said, arranging a display of paperback books. "It's all she talked about – how well Star has done at dog shows. It just seemed a lonely sort of life."

Maddy stared after Ms Flint as she and Star disappeared behind the crafts tent. *Was* she lonely? Then she shook herself. Well, if she was, it was her own fault! Star would love to be her friend, but she didn't want anything to do with him.

He'll be much better off with Sophie, Maddy assured herself.

People seemed to start noticing their stall then, and the next few hours passed in a busy blur. Soon there were so many people on the green that Maddy couldn't tell whether Sophie had arrived or not. She was hugely relieved when Rachel finally came panting up. "Where have you been?" she hissed. "You said you'd be here at ten!"

"I know, I'm sorry!" said Rachel. "It took my parents ages to get ready. Is Sophie here yet?"

Maddy gave a frustrated grimace. "I don't know – there's so many people that I can't tell!"

"I'll go and see if I can find her," said Rachel, and dashed off again.

"One pound," said Mum to a man buying a pile of paperbacks. She smiled at Maddy. "Isn't this fun?"

Maddy nodded quickly. "Yes, it's great!" Nibs had become ceramic ages ago, and lay nestled in her jacket pocket. She touched the little cat's cool smoothness for comfort. Oh, their plan *had* to work – it just had to!

Soon Rachel came running back. "I don't see her anywhere," she whispered, leaning across the stall. "But, Maddy, you and Nibs have got to come. The dog show's about to start!"

Maddy's mouth went dry. "But if Sophie's not here—"

"She might be, I just can't tell in this crowd!" cried Rachel. "Maddy, you've *got* to come! What if she's here, and we don't go through with it?"

Maddy's thoughts whirled. Suddenly it all seemed to be happening too fast. "Um, Mum . . . can I go and get something to eat?" she asked, crossing her fingers tightly at her side.

Chapter Seven

Her mother thanked a customer, and then glanced at her watch. "Yes, it *is* about that time, isn't it?" She handed Maddy some money. "Here, you and Rachel go and get whatever you want. Then once you're back, I'll nip off and grab something."

"Thanks, Mum!" The two girls raced off, darting through the crowd. "I've got to find somewhere to turn shadowy," panted Maddy.

"In here!" Rachel pulled her into the shiny white Portakabin that held the temporary loos. Hurrying up the stairs, they crowded into a cubicle together. Maddy took a deep breath, summoning her cat magic. The tingling swept through her, and a moment later, she'd vanished from view.

Nibs came to life and climbed out of her pocket, shadowy as well. "Oh good, it's time," she purred, leaping invisibly onto Maddy's shoulder. "I'm looking forward to this!"

Maddy tried not to think about what Nibs might have in mind to make Star misbehave. Opening the cubicle door again, she slipped out, with Rachel behind her. A woman brushing her hair at the mirror stopped and stared.

"Excuse me . . . weren't there two of you in there just now?" she asked Rachel.

"No, just me," said Rachel.

The woman shook her head sharply. "That'll teach me to drink at lunch time," she muttered.

The two girls hurried down the steps. "Hold my hand so I don't lose you!" hissed Rachel. Holding hands tightly, they raced across the green. As they rounded the crafts tent, Maddy could see the ring set up for the dog show.

Her eyes widened. She'd never *seen* so many dogs! Big ones, little ones, fluffy ones, spotted ones – there must be dozens! They were all on leads, gathered around the edge of the ring with their owners. Ms Flint stood in the centre with Star, talking to the crowd.

Oh no! thought Maddy. The demonstration had already begun! She stuck close to Rachel as they pushed their way through the throng. When they reached the front, she scanned the crowd wildly. Sophie – where was Sophie?

Suddenly she spotted her, and almost shouted with relief. The dark-haired girl was standing on the other side of the ring with her parents, gazing in wonder at all the dogs.

"She's here," Maddy whispered to Rachel. "Look, near the Dalmatian!"

"Oh, phew!" Rachel's shoulders relaxed. Then she nudged Maddy hard. "What are you waiting for, then? Go on!"

With Nibs still on her shoulder, Maddy edged invisibly out into the open. It felt very strange to have so many people staring straight through her!

"Now, I'm going to demonstrate a

few moves with Star, and then show you a few simple commands that you can use with your dogs," Ms Flint was saying. Star sat at her side, head up, gazing straight ahead.

"Perfect! Put me on the ground," muttered Nibs in Maddy's ear.

Maddy gently placed the little cat on the grass. "Nibs . . . you're not going to *claw* Star to make him misbehave, are you?" she whispered.

"Why, the very idea!" said Nibs. There was a tiny rustle as she bounded away over the grass, and then nothing. Maddy stood up again, frowning as she realized Nibs hadn't answered the question.

"Star, *stay*," said Ms Flint. She strode away from him. Star sat where he was, not moving a muscle.

Ms Flint stopped about ten paces away. "Star, *come*," she said after a pause. Star leaped to his feet and began trotting over to her. About halfway there, he slowed, shaking his head . . . but then went on.

As Ms Flint went through a few other moves, Star continued to behave perfectly. Occasionally he'd hesitate slightly, but Maddy thought that if she hadn't been watching closely, she wouldn't even have noticed. She hugged herself anxiously. What was going on? Why wasn't he misbehaving?

After a few minutes Ms Flint finished, and the audience applauded. "Thank you." She smiled. "Now, let me show you a few things you can do—"

Maddy stifled a shriek as she felt Nibs scrambling up her jeans. She lifted her up quickly. "What happened?" she whispered.

"Bah!" spat Nibs. "Dogs with thick coats – there should be a law against it!"

"You *did* try to claw him," accused Maddy.

"Only a little." Nibs sulked. "I didn't *hurt* the great brute. He was supposed to go berserk and start tearing about the ring, but he barely even felt it! Then I tried reasoning with him, but he just ignored me. I think he still feels guilty about misbehaving in the woods that day."

"Oh, no!" breathed Maddy. "What are we going to do?"

"I don't know," admitted Nibs

sadly. "Unless *you* have any ideas."

Maddy looked around in desperation. The owners were all listening to Ms Flint as she explained how to make your dog stay. "First, a strong voice is essential," she said. "The dog must always know that *you* are the boss . . ."

Suddenly Maddy noticed a man with a chocolate lab in the crowd. There was a chewed tennis ball on the ground beside the dog, as if it had just dropped it.

An idea came to Maddy. She glanced at Star, who sat just as perfectly beside Ms Flint as before. Would he do it? She didn't know . . . but she had to try. This might be their only chance!

Chapter Eight

Tiptoeing invisibly into the ring, Maddy crouched down beside Star. She saw his nostrils twitch as he smelled her. "Hi, Star, it's me," she whispered. "Do you want to play?"

"The second thing is to *move with confidence*," Ms Flint was saying. "Dogs read body language, you know. You must be the leader of the pack – bold and strong!"

Maddy gently stroked Star's head. "Remember how great it was playing fetch together?" she hissed in his floppy ear. "Don't you want to play fetch with me again?"

The tip of Star's tail wagged, and Maddy knew he was remembering how much fun it had been playing fetch. It had probably been one of the few times he'd ever played, she thought. Well, with any luck, after today he'd have owners who would play with him every day!

"Now, all of *you* try," said Ms Flint. "Start by putting your dog in the *sit* position beside you."

"*Sit*," said dozens of owners. There was a rustling noise as most of their dogs obeyed.

Maddy glanced again at the ball beside the chocolate lab. "Do you see that ball over there?" she murmured to Star, gently turning his head so that he'd spot it. "Fetch, Star! Fetch the ball!"

"Now drop your leads," instructed Ms Flint. "Say *Stay* – strong voices, remember! And then take a few steps away."

"Stay!" commanded the owners, moving slowly away from their dogs.

Star glanced uncertainly up at Ms Flint. *Oh, please!* thought Maddy, her hands tightening into anxious fists. "Fetch!" she whispered again. "Go on, boy – *fetch*!"

All at once Star seemed to decide. Getting to his feet, he loped over to the chocolate lab, grabbed its ball, and headed back to Maddy.

The crowd burst out laughing as Star dropped the ball near Ms Flint's feet. "*Star!*" she gasped. "What — ?

Whose ball is—?" She didn't finish. Realizing with a bark what had happened, the chocolate lab came bounding over, trailing its lead.

Before it could reach the ball, Maddy quickly grabbed it and shoved it into her pocket, where it became invisible. The lab stopped short, staring blankly at the ground.

"Hey, where'd the ball go?"

someone called.

Ms Flint peered down in confusion. "Why – I don't know – it was here a second ago . . ."

"Star, I know you can follow my scent," whispered Maddy in his ear. "Come on, catch me if you can!" She took off around the ring. Star, barking happily, came racing after her. So did the chocolate lab, smelling its ball.

"Star! Star, *stop*!" shrieked Ms Flint. Star ignored her as he and Maddy played chase. His tail was wagging as if it would never stop. The laughter turned to howls of delight as the two dogs romped and frolicked about the ring.

Then, with a yelp, a tiny Jack Russell suddenly seemed to go berserk, darting into the ring and racing around in frenzied circles. As if this was the cue they'd been waiting for, the other dogs all surged forward, barking madly.

All at once it was chaos. Maddy pounded about the ring with dozens of dogs galloping after her, and owners racing after the dogs, shouting and grabbing fruitlessly at their trailing leads.

"Wait, wait!" screamed Ms Flint at the centre of it all. "We must use proper commands! We must— *Argh!*" She broke off as the dogs streamed past her. Star leaped around her joyfully, accidentally wrapping his lead round her legs. With a screech, she fell to the ground, waving her arms about.

Chapter Eight

Glancing over her shoulder as she ran, Maddy was half horrified and half delighted. *That should do it*, she thought with a gulp. There was no way that Ms Flint would still want Star after this!

Hoping it wouldn't be noticed in the madness, she took the ball out of her pocket. "Fetch!" she cried, throwing it as far away from the dogs as she could.

Then she turned and sprinted in the opposite direction, dropping to her hands and knees to crawl invisibly away from the crowd. When she was safely out of sight, she ducked behind a stall, made herself visible again, and ran back to the ring.

Rachel was looking for her. "Oh, Maddy! That was *wonderful*!" she cried, her eyes shining.

"Come on," panted Maddy. "We have to be there when Ms Flint decides she doesn't want Star any more, so we can tell her about Sophie's family!"

Only a few minutes had passed. The ring was still a madhouse, with dogs leaping about, and owners running after them. "Wow!" said a man as he dragged away an over-excited collie. "This is one dog show I'll certainly never forget."

Ms Flint was still sitting on the ground. "Oh! I have *never*, in all my born days . . . What a *disobedient*—"

Star lay down beside her, his big brown eyes filled with remorse.

As she spoke, he edged forward cautiously, laying his golden head on her knee.

Ms Flint didn't seem to notice. "I try to show everyone how well-trained my dog is – for my *obedience school*, no less – and he – and he . . ." Suddenly her shoulders were shaking. She buried her head in her hands.

Maddy bit her lip, feeling awful. She hadn't meant to make Ms Flint *cry*. She and Rachel shifted on their feet, looking uneasily at each other.

Star whined, nudging his head further into Ms Flint's lap. She raised her head with a wail – and Maddy's jaw dropped in astonishment. It was a wail of *laughter*! Ms Flint was actually laughing!

"Oh, Star!" she cried, wiping her

eyes with her sleeve. "Oh, my gosh!
I've never *seen* anything so funny!
You horrible dog, you!" But she had
flung her arms around his neck as she
said it, and was hugging him hard.
Star squirmed delightedly, barking
and licking her face.

Maddy stared. Could it be possible?

Pulling away, Ms Flint held Star's
face in her hands for a long moment,
staring into his eyes as if she'd never
seen him before. He gazed eagerly
back at her. "Come on, you lovely
boy," she said softly, getting to her
feet. "Let's go home."

Star leaped up joyfully, barking.
Then Ms Flint spotted Maddy
standing nearby. She shook her head.

"I might have known you'd be
here," she said with a smile. But it

was a very different smile to the one she'd given Maddy before. It made Maddy feel warm inside, and she smiled back at her.

"Hi, Ms Flint," she said.

Ms Flint cleared her throat. "I hate to admit this, but – but I think you may have been right about Star. Seeing him running and playing like that, and having such a good time . . . well, I can see now that he hasn't been happy." Her cheeks reddened. She looked down, stroking Star's silky head.

"You see, we always had champion dogs when I was growing up, and I think I got so caught up with winning that – that I forgot what having a dog is all about. It's about having a *friend*. Someone who can make you laugh,

or comfort you when you're feeling
down. But you reminded me, didn't
you, boy?" she said, swooping down
to give Star another hug. His tail
wagged as if it would never stop.

Ms Flint straightened up. "And you
reminded me too," she said to Maddy.
"You were right – he needs love, not
trophies. And I'll see that he gets it
from now on."

"I'm really glad," said Maddy shyly.
She was in a daze. She'd been right

all along – Ms Flint *did* care for Star!

A woman with a Dalmatian stopped. "Well, *that* was an exciting exhibition!" She laughed. "But I was very impressed with how Star obeyed your commands before all the fun started. When did you say your school will be starting up?"

As Ms Flint talked to the woman, a few other dog owners came forward to speak to her as well. Maddy and Rachel grinned at each other in delight. Not only had Ms Flint realized how she felt about her dog, but it looked like she'd still have her school too.

All at once Maddy felt a tug at her jeans. Looking down, she saw Nibs sitting on her trainer, gazing up at her. "Nibs!" she gasped. She hadn't even

noticed that the little cat was gone!

Ducking behind Rachel so that no one would see, Maddy carefully scooped Nibs up onto her palm. The cat looked very pleased with herself. "Well, *that* turned out to be rather fun after all!" she purred.

Maddy narrowed her eyes. "What do you mean? Nibs! That Jack Russell, the one that went mad and set all the other dogs off – that wasn't *you*, was it?"

"Why, I have no idea what you mean," said Nibs airily, beginning to wash herself.

Maddy started to say something else, and then heard a voice behind her. "Maddy! Maddy, guess what!"

Immediately Nibs became ceramic in her hand. Tucking the tiny cat into her jacket pocket, Maddy turned round and saw Sophie. She winced. She'd forgotten all about her!

"Oh, Sophie! Listen, I'm really sorry, but—" she started.

Sophie blinked. "Sorry? What for? Haven't you heard about the puppies?"

Maddy stared at her. "Um . . . what puppies?"

"The chocolate labs!" cried Sophie, giving an excited jump. "The chocolate lab in the show had puppies a few months ago, and the owners are trying to find homes for them all. Dad says we can go to their house tomorrow and have a look!"

Lucky Star

"*Really?*" gasped Rachel

"Sophie, that's great!" said Maddy at the same time.

The younger girl shook her head, looking confused. "But . . . I thought you knew," she said. "Isn't that why you told me to come here?"

Maddy couldn't meet Rachel's gaze, or she knew she'd start to giggle.

"Sort of," she said. "I'm really glad about the puppies, Sophie. I hope you get to have one."

"And on my birthday too!" said Sophie gleefully. "It's going to be the best birthday ever, I just know it!" Her parents called to her then, and she went running off, her dark hair flying.

Maddy and Rachel looked at each other and burst out laughing. Suddenly Maddy realized something, and her laughter dried up as abruptly as if she'd turned off a tap. "Oh, my gosh! Mum! Come on, Rachel, we have to get back."

But to Maddy's surprise, not nearly as much time had passed as she'd thought. Mum just looked up and smiled as they came racing back. "Did you get something to eat?"

Maddy's stomach rumbled at the reminder. "Well, not *exactly* . . ."

Mum shook her head with a groan. "You two! You've just been larking about, haven't you? Look, go and get some food, and then come *straight back*."

Maddy was only too happy to do what she was told. Suddenly she was starving!

The rest of the afternoon was spent selling items from the stall. Rachel helped, and the time flew by. But the best part of the day, Maddy thought, was when Ms Flint walked by with Star. He was practically prancing, his plumy tail waving in the air and his eyes glowing with joy. Ms Flint looked different too. She smiled at people as she passed, and seemed relaxed and happy.

Mum gave a friendly nod as Ms Flint waved at them. "Well, she looks pleased with herself, doesn't she? Her exhibition must have gone really well."

Looking sideways at each other, Maddy and Rachel spluttered with laughter. Star glanced back at them, wagging his tail and giving a doggy grin. Maddy felt so happy that she thought her heart would burst. They'd done it. They'd really done it!

Then her smile faded as she remembered: Star had an owner who loved him now . . . and that meant the problem was solved.

Nibs would be leaving soon.

"It's almost time, Maddy," said Nibs.

It was late that evening, and the little cat had just returned from her nightly prowl. She jumped down from the windowsill to the bed, landing on the duvet so lightly that she didn't even dent it.

Maddy had been sitting up waiting for her. She nodded, and tried to smile. "I know," she whispered. No matter how many times she had to say goodbye to the little cats after her adventures with them, it didn't get any easier.

Nibs sprang onto her knee, no larger than a mouse. "Don't be sad," she said. "We solved the problem, didn't we? Even if it did involve a *dog*." She gave a disgusted shiver, and Maddy laughed despite everything.

"I don't think you really hated him at all," she said.

Nibs rolled her eyes. "Oh, all right," she said. "If you're going to make me admit it, then I suppose he wasn't *quite* as slobbering or as clumsy as some dogs I've known. But his breath really was awful."

Maddy smiled, and stretched out her hand so that Nibs could climb onto it. She cuddled the little cat against her chest for a long time, scratching under her chin and stroking her glossy black fur as Nibs purred.

Finally Nibs rubbed her head against Maddy's fingers. "I'm afraid it's time," she said gently.

Fighting back the tears, Maddy carried Nibs over to the desk where Greykin and Ollie waited. Nibs hopped down. "Goodbye, dear one," she said. "You did a good job. Just think of how happy we've made Fido!" Her green eyes gleamed.

"I know." Maddy nodded, and even through her sadness, she knew that seeing Star and Ms Flint together would give her a warm glow inside for a long time to come.

Nibs nuzzled her head once more against Maddy's hand. Then she walked slowly across the desk, the lamp casting a long cat shadow behind her. She settled herself beside

Greykin, and gave him a hard look.

"Yes, an interesting adventure indeed – ha, ha." She sniffed, entwining her tail with his.

"Goodbye," choked out Maddy. "I'll see you soon, I hope."

"Goodbye, Maddy," said Nibs with a narrow-eyed feline smile. "Until next time, my dear."

She sat very still, and then, as Maddy watched, her small, furry body seemed to shimmer. A moment later she sat frozen beside the other cats, as hard and ceramic as them.

Maddy sighed, and touched Nibs's smooth head. She'd forgotten to ask how long it might be before her next adventure. What if it was months and months again? But even as she thought it, she knew that it didn't matter. The cats' magic was real . . . and it was hers. She could wait for as long as it took.

"Goodbye for now," said Maddy, stroking all three cats with her hand. "I can hardly wait until next time . . . whenever that might be!"

THE END

The
Goddesses